Merlin And Vivien

Alfred Lord Tennyson

© 2023 Culturea Editions
Texte et illustration de couverture : © domaine public
Edition : Culturea (Hérault, 34)
Contact : infos@culturea.fr
Retrouvez notre catalogue sur http://culturea.fr
Imprimé en Allemagne par Books on Demand
Design typographique : Derek Murphy
Layout : Reedsy (https://reedsy.com/)
ISBN : 9791041817559
Dépôt légal : Juin 2023
Tous droits réservés pour tous pays

Merlin And Vivien

A storm was coming, but the winds were still,
And in the wild woods of Broceliande,
Before an oak, so hollow, huge and old
It looked a tower of ivied masonwork,
At Merlin's feet the wily Vivien lay.

For he that always bare in bitter grudge
The slights of Arthur and his Table, Mark
The Cornish King, had heard a wandering voice,
A minstrel of Caerlon by strong storm
Blown into shelter at Tintagil, say
That out of naked knightlike purity
Sir Lancelot worshipt no unmarried girl
But the great Queen herself, fought in her name,
Sware by her--vows like theirs, that high in heaven
Love most, but neither marry, nor are given
In marriage, angels of our Lord's report.

He ceased, and then--for Vivien sweetly said
(She sat beside the banquet nearest Mark),
'And is the fair example followed, Sir,
In Arthur's household?'--answered innocently:

'Ay, by some few--ay, truly--youths that hold
It more beseems the perfect virgin knight
To worship woman as true wife beyond
All hopes of gaining, than as maiden girl.
They place their pride in Lancelot and the Queen.
So passionate for an utter purity
Beyond the limit of their bond, are these,
For Arthur bound them not to singleness.
Brave hearts and clean! and yet--God guide them--
young.'

Then Mark was half in heart to hurl his cup
Straight at the speaker, but forbore: he rose
To leave the hall, and, Vivien following him,
Turned to her: 'Here are snakes within the grass;

And you methinks, O Vivien, save ye fear
The monkish manhood, and the mask of pure
Worn by this court, can stir them till they sting.'

And Vivien answered, smiling scornfully,
'Why fear? because that fostered at THY court
I savour of thy--virtues? fear them? no.
As Love, if Love is perfect, casts out fear,
So Hate, if Hate is perfect, casts out fear.
My father died in battle against the King,
My mother on his corpse in open field;
She bore me there, for born from death was I
Among the dead and sown upon the wind--
And then on thee! and shown the truth betimes,
That old true filth, and bottom of the well
Where Truth is hidden. Gracious lessons thine
And maxims of the mud! "This Arthur pure!
Great Nature through the flesh herself hath made
Gives him the lie! There is no being pure,
My cherub; saith not Holy Writ the same?"--
If I were Arthur, I would have thy blood.
Thy blessing, stainless King! I bring thee back,
When I have ferreted out their burrowings,
The hearts of all this Order in mine hand--
Ay--so that fate and craft and folly close,
Perchance, one curl of Arthur's golden beard.
To me this narrow grizzled fork of thine
Is cleaner-fashioned--Well, I loved thee first,
That warps the wit.'

Loud laughed the graceless Mark,
But Vivien, into Camelot stealing, lodged
Low in the city, and on a festal day
When Guinevere was crossing the great hall
Cast herself down, knelt to the Queen, and wailed.

'Why kneel ye there? What evil hath ye wrought?
Rise!' and the damsel bidden rise arose
And stood with folded hands and downward eyes
Of glancing corner, and all meekly said,

'None wrought, but suffered much, an orphan maid!
My father died in battle for thy King,
My mother on his corpse--in open field,
The sad sea-sounding wastes of Lyonnesse--
Poor wretch--no friend!--and now by Mark the King
For that small charm of feature mine, pursued--
If any such be mine--I fly to thee.
Save, save me thou--Woman of women--thine
The wreath of beauty, thine the crown of power,
Be thine the balm of pity, O Heaven's own white
Earth-angel, stainless bride of stainless King--
Help, for he follows! take me to thyself!
O yield me shelter for mine innocency
Among thy maidens!

Here her slow sweet eyes
Fear-tremulous, but humbly hopeful, rose
Fixt on her hearer's, while the Queen who stood
All glittering like May sunshine on May leaves
In green and gold, and plumed with green replied,
'Peace, child! of overpraise and overblame
We choose the last. Our noble Arthur, him
Ye scarce can overpraise, will hear and know.
Nay--we believe all evil of thy Mark--
Well, we shall test thee farther; but this hour
We ride a-hawking with Sir Lancelot.
He hath given us a fair falcon which he trained;
We go to prove it. Bide ye here the while.'

She past; and Vivien murmured after 'Go!
I bide the while.' Then through the portal-arch
Peering askance, and muttering broken-wise,
As one that labours with an evil dream,
Beheld the Queen and Lancelot get to horse.

'Is that the Lancelot? goodly--ay, but gaunt:
Courteous--amends for gauntness--takes her hand--
That glance of theirs, but for the street, had been
A clinging kiss--how hand lingers in hand!
Let go at last!--they ride away--to hawk

For waterfowl. Royaller game is mine.
For such a supersensual sensual bond
As that gray cricket chirpt of at our hearth--
Touch flax with flame--a glance will serve--the liars!
Ah little rat that borest in the dyke
Thy hole by night to let the boundless deep
Down upon far-off cities while they dance--
Or dream--of thee they dreamed not--nor of me
These--ay, but each of either: ride, and dream
The mortal dream that never yet was mine--
Ride, ride and dream until ye wake--to me!
Then, narrow court and lubber King, farewell!
For Lancelot will be gracious to the rat,
And our wise Queen, if knowing that I know,
Will hate, loathe, fear--but honour me the more.'

Yet while they rode together down the plain,
Their talk was all of training, terms of art,
Diet and seeling, jesses, leash and lure.
'She is too noble' he said 'to check at pies,
Nor will she rake: there is no baseness in her.'
Here when the Queen demanded as by chance
'Know ye the stranger woman?' 'Let her be,'
Said Lancelot and unhooded casting off
The goodly falcon free; she towered; her bells,
Tone under tone, shrilled; and they lifted up
Their eager faces, wondering at the strength,
Boldness and royal knighthood of the bird
Who pounced her quarry and slew it. Many a time
As once--of old--among the flowers--they rode.

But Vivien half-forgotten of the Queen
Among her damsels broidering sat, heard, watched
And whispered: through the peaceful court she crept
And whispered: then as Arthur in the highest
Leavened the world, so Vivien in the lowest,
Arriving at a time of golden rest,
And sowing one ill hint from ear to ear,
While all the heathen lay at Arthur's feet,
And no quest came, but all was joust and play,

Leavened his hall. They heard and let her be.

Thereafter as an enemy that has left
Death in the living waters, and withdrawn,
The wily Vivien stole from Arthur's court.

She hated all the knights, and heard in thought
Their lavish comment when her name was named.
For once, when Arthur walking all alone,
Vext at a rumour issued from herself
Of some corruption crept among his knights,
Had met her, Vivien, being greeted fair,
Would fain have wrought upon his cloudy mood
With reverent eyes mock-loyal, shaken voice,
And fluttered adoration, and at last
With dark sweet hints of some who prized him more
Than who should prize him most; at which the King
Had gazed upon her blankly and gone by:
But one had watched, and had not held his peace:
It made the laughter of an afternoon
That Vivien should attempt the blameless King.
And after that, she set herself to gain
Him, the most famous man of all those times,
Merlin, who knew the range of all their arts,
Had built the King his havens, ships, and halls,
Was also Bard, and knew the starry heavens;
The people called him Wizard; whom at first
She played about with slight and sprightly talk,
And vivid smiles, and faintly-venomed points
Of slander, glancing here and grazing there;
And yielding to his kindlier moods, the Seer
Would watch her at her petulance, and play,
Even when they seemed unloveable, and laugh
As those that watch a kitten; thus he grew
Tolerant of what he half disdained, and she,
Perceiving that she was but half disdained,
Began to break her sports with graver fits,
Turn red or pale, would often when they met
Sigh fully, or all-silent gaze upon him
With such a fixt devotion, that the old man,

Though doubtful, felt the flattery, and at times
Would flatter his own wish in age for love,
And half believe her true: for thus at times
He wavered; but that other clung to him,
Fixt in her will, and so the seasons went.

Then fell on Merlin a great melancholy;
He walked with dreams and darkness, and he found
A doom that ever poised itself to fall,
An ever-moaning battle in the mist,
World-war of dying flesh against the life,
Death in all life and lying in all love,
The meanest having power upon the highest,
And the high purpose broken by the worm.

So leaving Arthur's court he gained the beach;
There found a little boat, and stept into it;
And Vivien followed, but he marked her not.
She took the helm and he the sail; the boat
Drave with a sudden wind across the deeps,
And touching Breton sands, they disembarked.
And then she followed Merlin all the way,
Even to the wild woods of Broceliande.
For Merlin once had told her of a charm,
The which if any wrought on anyone
With woven paces and with waving arms,
The man so wrought on ever seemed to lie
Closed in the four walls of a hollow tower,
From which was no escape for evermore;
And none could find that man for evermore,
Nor could he see but him who wrought the charm
Coming and going, and he lay as dead
And lost to life and use and name and fame.
And Vivien ever sought to work the charm
Upon the great Enchanter of the Time,
As fancying that her glory would be great
According to his greatness whom she quenched.

There lay she all her length and kissed his feet,
As if in deepest reverence and in love.

A twist of gold was round her hair; a robe
Of samite without price, that more exprest
Than hid her, clung about her lissome limbs,
In colour like the satin-shining palm
On sallows in the windy gleams of March:
And while she kissed them, crying, 'Trample me,
Dear feet, that I have followed through the world,
And I will pay you worship; tread me down
And I will kiss you for it;' he was mute:
So dark a forethought rolled about his brain,
As on a dull day in an Ocean cave
The blind wave feeling round his long sea-hall
In silence: wherefore, when she lifted up
A face of sad appeal, and spake and said,
'O Merlin, do ye love me?' and again,
'O Merlin, do ye love me?' and once more,
'Great Master, do ye love me?' he was mute.
And lissome Vivien, holding by his heel,
Writhed toward him, slided up his knee and sat,
Behind his ankle twined her hollow feet
Together, curved an arm about his neck,
Clung like a snake; and letting her left hand
Droop from his mighty shoulder, as a leaf,
Made with her right a comb of pearl to part
The lists of such a board as youth gone out
Had left in ashes: then he spoke and said,
Not looking at her, 'Who are wise in love
Love most, say least,' and Vivien answered quick,
'I saw the little elf-god eyeless once
In Arthur's arras hall at Camelot:
But neither eyes nor tongue--O stupid child!
Yet you are wise who say it; let me think
Silence is wisdom: I am silent then,
And ask no kiss;' then adding all at once,
'And lo, I clothe myself with wisdom,' drew
The vast and shaggy mantle of his beard
Across her neck and bosom to her knee,
And called herself a gilded summer fly
Caught in a great old tyrant spider's web,
Who meant to eat her up in that wild wood

Without one word. So Vivien called herself,
But rather seemed a lovely baleful star
Veiled in gray vapour; till he sadly smiled:
'To what request for what strange boon,' he said,
'Are these your pretty tricks and fooleries,
O Vivien, the preamble? yet my thanks,
For these have broken up my melancholy.'

And Vivien answered smiling saucily,
'What, O my Master, have ye found your voice?
I bid the stranger welcome. Thanks at last!
But yesterday you never opened lip,
Except indeed to drink: no cup had we:
In mine own lady palms I culled the spring
That gathered trickling dropwise from the cleft,
And made a pretty cup of both my hands
And offered you it kneeling: then you drank
And knew no more, nor gave me one poor word;
O no more thanks than might a goat have given
With no more sign of reverence than a beard.
And when we halted at that other well,
And I was faint to swooning, and you lay
Foot-gilt with all the blossom-dust of those
Deep meadows we had traversed, did you know
That Vivien bathed your feet before her own?
And yet no thanks: and all through this wild wood
And all this morning when I fondled you:
Boon, ay, there was a boon, one not so strange--
How had I wronged you? surely ye are wise,
But such a silence is more wise than kind.'

And Merlin locked his hand in hers and said:
'O did ye never lie upon the shore,
And watch the curled white of the coming wave
Glassed in the slippery sand before it breaks?
Even such a wave, but not so pleasurable,
Dark in the glass of some presageful mood,
Had I for three days seen, ready to fall.
And then I rose and fled from Arthur's court
To break the mood. You followed me unasked;

And when I looked, and saw you following me still,
My mind involved yourself the nearest thing
In that mind-mist: for shall I tell you truth?
You seemed that wave about to break upon me
And sweep me from my hold upon the world,
My use and name and fame. Your pardon, child.
Your pretty sports have brightened all again.
And ask your boon, for boon I owe you thrice,
Once for wrong done you by confusion, next
For thanks it seems till now neglected, last
For these your dainty gambols: wherefore ask;
And take this boon so strange and not so strange.'

And Vivien answered smiling mournfully:
'O not so strange as my long asking it,
Not yet so strange as you yourself are strange,
Nor half so strange as that dark mood of yours.
I ever feared ye were not wholly mine;
And see, yourself have owned ye did me wrong.
The people call you prophet: let it be:
But not of those that can expound themselves.
Take Vivien for expounder; she will call
That three-days-long presageful gloom of yours
No presage, but the same mistrustful mood
That makes you seem less noble than yourself,
Whenever I have asked this very boon,
Now asked again: for see you not, dear love,
That such a mood as that, which lately gloomed
Your fancy when ye saw me following you,
Must make me fear still more you are not mine,
Must make me yearn still more to prove you mine,
And make me wish still more to learn this charm
Of woven paces and of waving hands,
As proof of trust. O Merlin, teach it me.
The charm so taught will charm us both to rest.
For, grant me some slight power upon your fate,
I, feeling that you felt me worthy trust,
Should rest and let you rest, knowing you mine.
And therefore be as great as ye are named,
Not muffled round with selfish reticence.

How hard you look and how denyingly!
O, if you think this wickedness in me,
That I should prove it on you unawares,
That makes me passing wrathful; then our bond
Had best be loosed for ever: but think or not,
By Heaven that hears I tell you the clean truth,
As clean as blood of babes, as white as milk:
O Merlin, may this earth, if ever I,
If these unwitty wandering wits of mine,
Even in the jumbled rubbish of a dream,
Have tript on such conjectural treachery--
May this hard earth cleave to the Nadir hell
Down, down, and close again, and nip me flat,
If I be such a traitress. Yield my boon,
Till which I scarce can yield you all I am;
And grant my re-reiterated wish,
The great proof of your love: because I think,
However wise, ye hardly know me yet.'

And Merlin loosed his hand from hers and said,
'I never was less wise, however wise,
Too curious Vivien, though you talk of trust,
Than when I told you first of such a charm.
Yea, if ye talk of trust I tell you this,
Too much I trusted when I told you that,
And stirred this vice in you which ruined man
Through woman the first hour; for howsoe'er
In children a great curiousness be well,
Who have to learn themselves and all the world,
In you, that are no child, for still I find
Your face is practised when I spell the lines,
I call it,--well, I will not call it vice:
But since you name yourself the summer fly,
I well could wish a cobweb for the gnat,
That settles, beaten back, and beaten back
Settles, till one could yield for weariness:
But since I will not yield to give you power
Upon my life and use and name and fame,
Why will ye never ask some other boon?
Yea, by God's rood, I trusted you too much.'

10

And Vivien, like the tenderest-hearted maid
That ever bided tryst at village stile,
Made answer, either eyelid wet with tears:
'Nay, Master, be not wrathful with your maid;
Caress her: let her feel herself forgiven
Who feels no heart to ask another boon.
I think ye hardly know the tender rhyme
Of "trust me not at all or all in all."
I heard the great Sir Lancelot sing it once,
And it shall answer for me. Listen to it.

"In Love, if Love be Love, if Love be ours,
Faith and unfaith can ne'er be equal powers:
Unfaith in aught is want of faith in all.

"It is the little rift within the lute,
That by and by will make the music mute,
And ever widening slowly silence all.

"The little rift within the lover's lute
Or little pitted speck in garnered fruit,
That rotting inward slowly moulders all.

"It is not worth the keeping: let it go:
But shall it? answer, darling, answer, no.
And trust me not at all or all in all."

O Master, do ye love my tender rhyme?'

And Merlin looked and half believed her true,
So tender was her voice, so fair her face,
So sweetly gleamed her eyes behind her tears
Like sunlight on the plain behind a shower:
And yet he answered half indignantly:

'Far other was the song that once I heard
By this huge oak, sung nearly where we sit:
For here we met, some ten or twelve of us,
To chase a creature that was current then

In these wild woods, the hart with golden horns.
It was the time when first the question rose
About the founding of a Table Round,
That was to be, for love of God and men
And noble deeds, the flower of all the world.
And each incited each to noble deeds.
And while we waited, one, the youngest of us,
We could not keep him silent, out he flashed,
And into such a song, such fire for fame,
Such trumpet-glowings in it, coming down
To such a stern and iron-clashing close,
That when he stopt we longed to hurl together,
And should have done it; but the beauteous beast
Scared by the noise upstarted at our feet,
And like a silver shadow slipt away
Through the dim land; and all day long we rode
Through the dim land against a rushing wind,
That glorious roundel echoing in our ears,
And chased the flashes of his golden horns
Till they vanished by the fairy well
That laughs at iron--as our warriors did--
Where children cast their pins and nails, and cry,
"Laugh, little well!" but touch it with a sword,
It buzzes fiercely round the point; and there
We lost him: such a noble song was that.
But, Vivien, when you sang me that sweet rhyme,
I felt as though you knew this cursd charm,
Were proving it on me, and that I lay
And felt them slowly ebbing, name and fame.'

And Vivien answered smiling mournfully:
'O mine have ebbed away for evermore,
And all through following you to this wild wood,
Because I saw you sad, to comfort you.
Lo now, what hearts have men! they never mount
As high as woman in her selfless mood.
And touching fame, howe'er ye scorn my song,
Take one verse more--the lady speaks it--this:

'"My name, once mine, now thine, is closelier mine,

For fame, could fame be mine, that fame were thine,
And shame, could shame be thine, that shame were mine.
So trust me not at all or all in all."

'Says she not well? and there is more--this rhyme
Is like the fair pearl-necklace of the Queen,
That burst in dancing, and the pearls were spilt;
Some lost, some stolen, some as relics kept.
But nevermore the same two sister pearls
Ran down the silken thread to kiss each other
On her white neck--so is it with this rhyme:
It lives dispersedly in many hands,
And every minstrel sings it differently;
Yet is there one true line, the pearl of pearls:
"Man dreams of Fame while woman wakes to love."
Yea! Love, though Love were of the grossest, carves
A portion from the solid present, eats
And uses, careless of the rest; but Fame,
The Fame that follows death is nothing to us;
And what is Fame in life but half-disfame,
And counterchanged with darkness? ye yourself
Know well that Envy calls you Devil's son,
And since ye seem the Master of all Art,
They fain would make you Master of all vice.'

And Merlin locked his hand in hers and said,
'I once was looking for a magic weed,
And found a fair young squire who sat alone,
Had carved himself a knightly shield of wood,
And then was painting on it fancied arms,
Azure, an Eagle rising or, the Sun
In dexter chief; the scroll "I follow fame."
And speaking not, but leaning over him
I took his brush and blotted out the bird,
And made a Gardener putting in a graff,
With this for motto, "Rather use than fame."
You should have seen him blush; but afterwards
He made a stalwart knight. O Vivien,
For you, methinks you think you love me well;
For me, I love you somewhat; rest: and Love

Should have some rest and pleasure in himself,
Not ever be too curious for a boon,
Too prurient for a proof against the grain
Of him ye say ye love: but Fame with men,
Being but ampler means to serve mankind,
Should have small rest or pleasure in herself,
But work as vassal to the larger love,
That dwarfs the petty love of one to one.
Use gave me Fame at first, and Fame again
Increasing gave me use. Lo, there my boon!
What other? for men sought to prove me vile,
Because I fain had given them greater wits:
And then did Envy call me Devil's son:
The sick weak beast seeking to help herself
By striking at her better, missed, and brought
Her own claw back, and wounded her own heart.
Sweet were the days when I was all unknown,
But when my name was lifted up, the storm
Brake on the mountain and I cared not for it.
Right well know I that Fame is half-disfame,
Yet needs must work my work. That other fame,
To one at least, who hath not children, vague,
The cackle of the unborn about the grave,
I cared not for it: a single misty star,
Which is the second in a line of stars
That seem a sword beneath a belt of three,
I never gazed upon it but I dreamt
Of some vast charm concluded in that star
To make fame nothing. Wherefore, if I fear,
Giving you power upon me through this charm,
That you might play me falsely, having power,
However well ye think ye love me now
(As sons of kings loving in pupilage
Have turned to tyrants when they came to power)
I rather dread the loss of use than fame;
If you--and not so much from wickedness,
As some wild turn of anger, or a mood
Of overstrained affection, it may be,
To keep me all to your own self,--or else
A sudden spurt of woman's jealousy,--

Should try this charm on whom ye say ye love.'

And Vivien answered smiling as in wrath:
'Have I not sworn? I am not trusted. Good!
Well, hide it, hide it; I shall find it out;
And being found take heed of Vivien.
A woman and not trusted, doubtless I
Might feel some sudden turn of anger born
Of your misfaith; and your fine epithet
Is accurate too, for this full love of mine
Without the full heart back may merit well
Your term of overstrained. So used as I,
My daily wonder is, I love at all.
And as to woman's jealousy, O why not?
O to what end, except a jealous one,
And one to make me jealous if I love,
Was this fair charm invented by yourself?
I well believe that all about this world
Ye cage a buxom captive here and there,
Closed in the four walls of a hollow tower
From which is no escape for evermore.'

Then the great Master merrily answered her:
'Full many a love in loving youth was mine;
I needed then no charm to keep them mine
But youth and love; and that full heart of yours
Whereof ye prattle, may now assure you mine;
So live uncharmed. For those who wrought it first,
The wrist is parted from the hand that waved,
The feet unmortised from their ankle-bones
Who paced it, ages back: but will ye hear
The legend as in guerdon for your rhyme?

'There lived a king in the most Eastern East,
Less old than I, yet older, for my blood
Hath earnest in it of far springs to be.
A tawny pirate anchored in his port,
Whose bark had plundered twenty nameless isles;
And passing one, at the high peep of dawn,
He saw two cities in a thousand boats

All fighting for a woman on the sea.
And pushing his black craft among them all,
He lightly scattered theirs and brought her off,
With loss of half his people arrow-slain;
A maid so smooth, so white, so wonderful,
They said a light came from her when she moved:
And since the pirate would not yield her up,
The King impaled him for his piracy;
Then made her Queen: but those isle-nurtured eyes
Waged such unwilling though successful war
On all the youth, they sickened; councils thinned,
And armies waned, for magnet-like she drew
The rustiest iron of old fighters' hearts;
And beasts themselves would worship; camels knelt
Unbidden, and the brutes of mountain back
That carry kings in castles, bowed black knees
Of homage, ringing with their serpent hands,
To make her smile, her golden ankle-bells.
What wonder, being jealous, that he sent
His horns of proclamation out through all
The hundred under-kingdoms that he swayed
To find a wizard who might teach the King
Some charm, which being wrought upon the Queen
Might keep her all his own: to such a one
He promised more than ever king has given,
A league of mountain full of golden mines,
A province with a hundred miles of coast,
A palace and a princess, all for him:
But on all those who tried and failed, the King
Pronounced a dismal sentence, meaning by it
To keep the list low and pretenders back,
Or like a king, not to be trifled with--
Their heads should moulder on the city gates.
And many tried and failed, because the charm
Of nature in her overbore their own:
And many a wizard brow bleached on the walls:
And many weeks a troop of carrion crows
Hung like a cloud above the gateway towers.'

And Vivien breaking in upon him, said:

'I sit and gather honey; yet, methinks,
Thy tongue has tript a little: ask thyself.
The lady never made UNWILLING war
With those fine eyes: she had her pleasure in it,
And made her good man jealous with good cause.
And lived there neither dame nor damsel then
Wroth at a lover's loss? were all as tame,
I mean, as noble, as the Queen was fair?
Not one to flirt a venom at her eyes,
Or pinch a murderous dust into her drink,
Or make her paler with a poisoned rose?
Well, those were not our days: but did they find
A wizard? Tell me, was he like to thee?

She ceased, and made her lithe arm round his neck
Tighten, and then drew back, and let her eyes
Speak for her, glowing on him, like a bride's
On her new lord, her own, the first of men.

He answered laughing, 'Nay, not like to me.
At last they found--his foragers for charms--
A little glassy-headed hairless man,
Who lived alone in a great wild on grass;
Read but one book, and ever reading grew
So grated down and filed away with thought,
So lean his eyes were monstrous; while the skin
Clung but to crate and basket, ribs and spine.
And since he kept his mind on one sole aim,
Nor ever touched fierce wine, nor tasted flesh,
Nor owned a sensual wish, to him the wall
That sunders ghosts and shadow-casting men
Became a crystal, and he saw them through it,
And heard their voices talk behind the wall,
And learnt their elemental secrets, powers
And forces; often o'er the sun's bright eye
Drew the vast eyelid of an inky cloud,
And lashed it at the base with slanting storm;
Or in the noon of mist and driving rain,
When the lake whitened and the pinewood roared,
And the cairned mountain was a shadow, sunned

The world to peace again: here was the man.
And so by force they dragged him to the King.
And then he taught the King to charm the Queen
In such-wise, that no man could see her more,
Nor saw she save the King, who wrought the charm,
Coming and going, and she lay as dead,
And lost all use of life: but when the King
Made proffer of the league of golden mines,
The province with a hundred miles of coast,
The palace and the princess, that old man
Went back to his old wild, and lived on grass,
And vanished, and his book came down to me.'

And Vivien answered smiling saucily:
'Ye have the book: the charm is written in it:
Good: take my counsel: let me know it at once:
For keep it like a puzzle chest in chest,
With each chest locked and padlocked thirty-fold,
And whelm all this beneath as vast a mound
As after furious battle turfs the slain
On some wild down above the windy deep,
I yet should strike upon a sudden means
To dig, pick, open, find and read the charm:
Then, if I tried it, who should blame me then?'

And smiling as a master smiles at one
That is not of his school, nor any school
But that where blind and naked Ignorance
Delivers brawling judgments, unashamed,
On all things all day long, he answered her:

'Thou read the book, my pretty Vivien!
O ay, it is but twenty pages long,
But every page having an ample marge,
And every marge enclosing in the midst
A square of text that looks a little blot,
The text no larger than the limbs of fleas;
And every square of text an awful charm,
Writ in a language that has long gone by.
So long, that mountains have arisen since

With cities on their flanks--thou read the book!
And ever margin scribbled, crost, and crammed
With comment, densest condensation, hard
To mind and eye; but the long sleepless nights
Of my long life have made it easy to me.
And none can read the text, not even I;
And none can read the comment but myself;
And in the comment did I find the charm.
O, the results are simple; a mere child
Might use it to the harm of anyone,
And never could undo it: ask no more:
For though you should not prove it upon me,
But keep that oath ye sware, ye might, perchance,
Assay it on some one of the Table Round,
And all because ye dream they babble of you.'

And Vivien, frowning in true anger, said:
'What dare the full-fed liars say of me?
THEY ride abroad redressing human wrongs!
They sit with knife in meat and wine in horn!
THEY bound to holy vows of chastity!
Were I not woman, I could tell a tale.
But you are man, you well can understand
The shame that cannot be explained for shame.
Not one of all the drove should touch me: swine!'

Then answered Merlin careless of her words:
'You breathe but accusation vast and vague,
Spleen-born, I think, and proofless. If ye know,
Set up the charge ye know, to stand or fall!'

And Vivien answered frowning wrathfully:
'O ay, what say ye to Sir Valence, him
Whose kinsman left him watcher o'er his wife
And two fair babes, and went to distant lands;
Was one year gone, and on returning found
Not two but three? there lay the reckling, one
But one hour old! What said the happy sire?'
A seven-months' babe had been a truer gift.
Those twelve sweet moons confused his fatherhood.'

Then answered Merlin, 'Nay, I know the tale.
Sir Valence wedded with an outland dame:
Some cause had kept him sundered from his wife:
One child they had: it lived with her: she died:
His kinsman travelling on his own affair
Was charged by Valence to bring home the child.
He brought, not found it therefore: take the truth.'

'O ay,' said Vivien, 'overtrue a tale.
What say ye then to sweet Sir Sagramore,
That ardent man? "to pluck the flower in season,"
So says the song, "I trow it is no treason."
O Master, shall we call him overquick
To crop his own sweet rose before the hour?'

And Merlin answered, 'Overquick art thou
To catch a loathly plume fallen from the wing
Of that foul bird of rapine whose whole prey
Is man's good name: he never wronged his bride.
I know the tale. An angry gust of wind
Puffed out his torch among the myriad-roomed
And many-corridored complexities
Of Arthur's palace: then he found a door,
And darkling felt the sculptured ornament
That wreathen round it made it seem his own;
And wearied out made for the couch and slept,
A stainless man beside a stainless maid;
And either slept, nor knew of other there;
Till the high dawn piercing the royal rose
In Arthur's casement glimmered chastely down,
Blushing upon them blushing, and at once
He rose without a word and parted from her:
But when the thing was blazed about the court,
The brute world howling forced them into bonds,
And as it chanced they are happy, being pure.'

'O ay,' said Vivien, 'that were likely too.
What say ye then to fair Sir Percivale
And of the horrid foulness that he wrought,

The saintly youth, the spotless lamb of Christ,
Or some black wether of St Satan's fold.
What, in the precincts of the chapel-yard,
Among the knightly brasses of the graves,
And by the cold Hic Jacets of the dead!'

And Merlin answered careless of her charge,
'A sober man is Percivale and pure;
But once in life was flustered with new wine,
Then paced for coolness in the chapel-yard;
Where one of Satan's shepherdesses caught
And meant to stamp him with her master's mark;
And that he sinned is not believable;
For, look upon his face!--but if he sinned,
The sin that practice burns into the blood,
And not the one dark hour which brings remorse,
Will brand us, after, of whose fold we be:
Or else were he, the holy king, whose hymns
Are chanted in the minster, worse than all.
But is your spleen frothed out, or have ye more?'

And Vivien answered frowning yet in wrath:
'O ay; what say ye to Sir Lancelot, friend
Traitor or true? that commerce with the Queen,
I ask you, is it clamoured by the child,
Or whispered in the corner? do ye know it?'

To which he answered sadly, 'Yea, I know it.
Sir Lancelot went ambassador, at first,
To fetch her, and she watched him from her walls.
A rumour runs, she took him for the King,
So fixt her fancy on him: let them be.
But have ye no one word of loyal praise
For Arthur, blameless King and stainless man?'

She answered with a low and chuckling laugh:
'Man! is he man at all, who knows and winks?
Sees what his fair bride is and does, and winks?
By which the good King means to blind himself,
And blinds himself and all the Table Round

To all the foulness that they work. Myself
Could call him (were it not for womanhood)
The pretty, popular cause such manhood earns,
Could call him the main cause of all their crime;
Yea, were he not crowned King, coward, and fool.'

Then Merlin to his own heart, loathing, said:
'O true and tender! O my liege and King!
O selfless man and stainless gentleman,
Who wouldst against thine own eye-witness fain
Have all men true and leal, all women pure;
How, in the mouths of base interpreters,
From over-fineness not intelligible
To things with every sense as false and foul
As the poached filth that floods the middle street,
Is thy white blamelessness accounted blame!'

But Vivien, deeming Merlin overborne
By instance, recommenced, and let her tongue
Rage like a fire among the noblest names,
Polluting, and imputing her whole self,
Defaming and defacing, till she left
Not even Lancelot brave, nor Galahad clean.

Her words had issue other than she willed.
He dragged his eyebrow bushes down, and made
A snowy penthouse for his hollow eyes,
And muttered in himself, 'Tell HER the charm!
So, if she had it, would she rail on me
To snare the next, and if she have it not
So will she rail. What did the wanton say?
"Not mount as high;" we scarce can sink as low:
For men at most differ as Heaven and earth,
But women, worst and best, as Heaven and Hell.
I know the Table Round, my friends of old;
All brave, and many generous, and some chaste.
She cloaks the scar of some repulse with lies;
I well believe she tempted them and failed,
Being so bitter: for fine plots may fail,
Though harlots paint their talk as well as face

With colours of the heart that are not theirs.
I will not let her know: nine tithes of times
Face-flatterer and backbiter are the same.
And they, sweet soul, that most impute a crime
Are pronest to it, and impute themselves,
Wanting the mental range; or low desire
Not to feel lowest makes them level all;
Yea, they would pare the mountain to the plain,
To leave an equal baseness; and in this
Are harlots like the crowd, that if they find
Some stain or blemish in a name of note,
Not grieving that their greatest are so small,
Inflate themselves with some insane delight,
And judge all nature from her feet of clay,
Without the will to lift their eyes, and see
Her godlike head crowned with spiritual fire,
And touching other worlds. I am weary of her.'

He spoke in words part heard, in whispers part,
Half-suffocated in the hoary fell
And many-wintered fleece of throat and chin.
But Vivien, gathering somewhat of his mood,
And hearing 'harlot' muttered twice or thrice,
Leapt from her session on his lap, and stood
Stiff as a viper frozen; loathsome sight,
How from the rosy lips of life and love,
Flashed the bare-grinning skeleton of death!
White was her cheek; sharp breaths of anger puffed
Her fairy nostril out; her hand half-clenched
Went faltering sideways downward to her belt,
And feeling; had she found a dagger there
(For in a wink the false love turns to hate)
She would have stabbed him; but she found it not:
His eye was calm, and suddenly she took
To bitter weeping like a beaten child,
A long, long weeping, not consolable.
Then her false voice made way, broken with sobs:

'O crueller than was ever told in tale,
Or sung in song! O vainly lavished love!

O cruel, there was nothing wild or strange,
Or seeming shameful--for what shame in love,
So love be true, and not as yours is--nothing
Poor Vivien had not done to win his trust
Who called her what he called her--all her crime,
All--all--the wish to prove him wholly hers.'

She mused a little, and then clapt her hands
Together with a wailing shriek, and said:
'Stabbed through the heart's affections to the heart!
Seethed like the kid in its own mother's milk!
Killed with a word worse than a life of blows!
I thought that he was gentle, being great:
O God, that I had loved a smaller man!
I should have found in him a greater heart.
O, I, that flattering my true passion, saw
The knights, the court, the King, dark in your light,
Who loved to make men darker than they are,
Because of that high pleasure which I had
To seat you sole upon my pedestal
Of worship--I am answered, and henceforth
The course of life that seemed so flowery to me
With you for guide and master, only you,
Becomes the sea-cliff pathway broken short,
And ending in a ruin--nothing left,
But into some low cave to crawl, and there,
If the wolf spare me, weep my life away,
Killed with inutterable unkindliness.'

She paused, she turned away, she hung her head,
The snake of gold slid from her hair, the braid
Slipt and uncoiled itself, she wept afresh,
And the dark wood grew darker toward the storm
In silence, while his anger slowly died
Within him, till he let his wisdom go
For ease of heart, and half believed her true:
Called her to shelter in the hollow oak,
'Come from the storm,' and having no reply,
Gazed at the heaving shoulder, and the face
Hand-hidden, as for utmost grief or shame;

Then thrice essayed, by tenderest-touching terms,
To sleek her ruffled peace of mind, in vain.
At last she let herself be conquered by him,
And as the cageling newly flown returns,
The seeming-injured simple-hearted thing
Came to her old perch back, and settled there.
There while she sat, half-falling from his knees,
Half-nestled at his heart, and since he saw
The slow tear creep from her closed eyelid yet,
About her, more in kindness than in love,
The gentle wizard cast a shielding arm.
But she dislinked herself at once and rose,
Her arms upon her breast across, and stood,
A virtuous gentlewoman deeply wronged,
Upright and flushed before him: then she said:

'There must now be no passages of love
Betwixt us twain henceforward evermore;
Since, if I be what I am grossly called,
What should be granted which your own gross heart
Would reckon worth the taking? I will go.
In truth, but one thing now--better have died
Thrice than have asked it once--could make me stay--
That proof of trust--so often asked in vain!
How justly, after that vile term of yours,
I find with grief! I might believe you then,
Who knows? once more. Lo! what was once to me
Mere matter of the fancy, now hath grown
The vast necessity of heart and life.
Farewell; think gently of me, for I fear
My fate or folly, passing gayer youth
For one so old, must be to love thee still.
But ere I leave thee let me swear once more
That if I schemed against thy peace in this,
May yon just heaven, that darkens o'er me, send
One flash, that, missing all things else, may make
My scheming brain a cinder, if I lie.'

Scarce had she ceased, when out of heaven a bolt
 (For now the storm was close above them) struck,

Furrowing a giant oak, and javelining
With darted spikes and splinters of the wood
The dark earth round. He raised his eyes and saw
The tree that shone white-listed through the gloom.
But Vivien, fearing heaven had heard her oath,
And dazzled by the livid-flickering fork,
And deafened with the stammering cracks and claps
That followed, flying back and crying out,
'O Merlin, though you do not love me, save,
Yet save me!' clung to him and hugged him close;
And called him dear protector in her fright,
Nor yet forgot her practice in her fright,
But wrought upon his mood and hugged him close.
The pale blood of the wizard at her touch
Took gayer colours, like an opal warmed.
She blamed herself for telling hearsay tales:
She shook from fear, and for her fault she wept
Of petulancy; she called him lord and liege,
Her seer, her bard, her silver star of eve,
Her God, her Merlin, the one passionate love
Of her whole life; and ever overhead
Bellowed the tempest, and the rotten branch
Snapt in the rushing of the river-rain
Above them; and in change of glare and gloom
Her eyes and neck glittering went and came;
Till now the storm, its burst of passion spent,
Moaning and calling out of other lands,
Had left the ravaged woodland yet once more
To peace; and what should not have been had been,
For Merlin, overtalked and overworn,
Had yielded, told her all the charm, and slept.

Then, in one moment, she put forth the charm
Of woven paces and of waving hands,
And in the hollow oak he lay as dead,
And lost to life and use and name and fame.

Then crying 'I have made his glory mine,'
And shrieking out 'O fool!' the harlot leapt

Adown the forest, and the thicket closed
Behind her, and the forest echoed 'fool.'

Milton (Alcaics)

O mighty-mouth'd inventor of harmonies,
O skill'd to sing of Time or Eternity,
God-gifted organ-voice of England,
Milton, a name to resound for ages;
Whose Titan angels, Gabriel, Abdiel,
Starr'd from Jehovah's gorgeous armouries,
Tower, as the deep-domed empyrean
Rings to the roar of an angel onset--
Me rather all that bowery loneliness,
The brooks of Eden mazily murmuring,
And bloom profuse and cedar arches
Charm, as a wanderer out in ocean,
Where some refulgent sunset of India
Streams o'er a rich ambrosial ocean isle,
And crimson-hued the stately palm-woods
Whisper in odorous heights of even.